THIS WALKER BOOK BELONGS TO:

_____

_____

_____

For all my friends
but especially for Carys, David and Helen,
who were there at the birth

To find out more about
Simon James and his books visit
www.simonjamesbooks.com

First published 2004 by Walker Books Ltd
87 Vauxhall Walk, London SE11 5HJ

This edition including DVD published 2007

2 4 6 8 10 9 7 5 3 1

This book has been typeset in Cochin

Printed in China

British Library Cataloguing in Publication Data:
a catalogue record for this book is
available from the British Library

ISBN 978-1-4063-0956-0

www.walkerbooks.co.uk

Baby *Brains

Simon James

WALKER BOOKS

AND SUBSIDIARIES

LONDON · BOSTON · SYDNEY · AUCKLAND

In the months
before Baby Brains
was born
Mrs Brains
was very busy.

She read out loud every night to the baby inside her tummy.

She played music and languages on headphones
to her baby during the day.
Mr and Mrs Brains wanted to make sure their baby
was going to be very clever.

They even turned up the television when the news came on.

Mr and Mrs Brains were very excited when
their baby was born. It was a boy.
"Our very own Baby Brains," said Mr Brains proudly.

When they brought him home from hospital
Mrs Brains laid him down in the brand-new cot.
"Sleep tight, Baby Brains," she whispered.

The next morning, Mrs Brains was on
her way to get breakfast when she heard some
strange noises in the living-room.

Mrs Brains opened the door to see her baby sitting
on the sofa, reading the morning paper.

By the afternoon Baby Brains was helping mend the car.
"We've certainly got a bright one here!" said Mr Brains.

That evening, Baby Brains spoke his first words…

"I'd like to go to school tomorrow," he said.

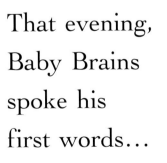

The next day Baby Brains visited the local school.
He sat down with the children and answered all
the questions. The children were amazed.

At the end of the afternoon the teacher thanked Baby Brains.
"I don't think I've ever learnt so much in one day," she said.

On the way home Baby Brains said he wanted to go
to university and study medicine.

After just two weeks Baby Brains began working
as a doctor at the local hospital. He was very popular
with all the staff and patients.

Word soon spread about the extraordinary Baby Brains.
Everyone wanted to meet him.

One night some
space scientists
phoned.
They asked if
Baby Brains
would like to
help with their
next space mission.

The following day Mr and Mrs Brains and
their baby travelled out to the space centre.
After training hard over the weekend …

Baby Brains waved goodbye to Mr and Mrs Brains
and blasted off into outer space.

Everyone in the world held their breath as they watched
Baby Brains take his first space walk.
"Tell us how you feel on this special occasion,"
radioed Ground Control.

Baby Brains looked up
at the vast starlit sky
above him.

He looked down at the
vast starlit sky
below him.

He looked at the whole
world in front of him
and mumbled something.

"We can't quite hear you," radioed Ground Control.
"Could you repeat that?"

"I want my mummy!"

wailed Baby Brains.

"That's enough!" Mrs Brains yelled to the
space controller.
"Bring my baby home right now!"

Baby Brains was flown home as quickly
as possible. He felt very embarrassed as
he stepped down from the hatch.

But, through the crowd of photographers and cameramen,
Mrs Brains came running.

"Our beautiful little baby," sighed Mrs Brains,
as she lifted him high into the air.
"Our brave little baby," said Mr Brains.
"Can we go home?" said Baby Brains.

At home
Mrs Brains gave
Baby Brains
a warm bath,

which made him
feel a lot better.

Mr Brains tickled
him, which made
him laugh.

And Mrs Brains sang Baby Brains to sleep.
Then they gently laid him down in the brand-new cot.

It was good to have their baby home again.
"Our very own Baby Brains," whispered Mrs Brains.

From that day on, Baby Brains
spent most of his time at
home doing the things that
most babies do.
Except, that is, at weekends …

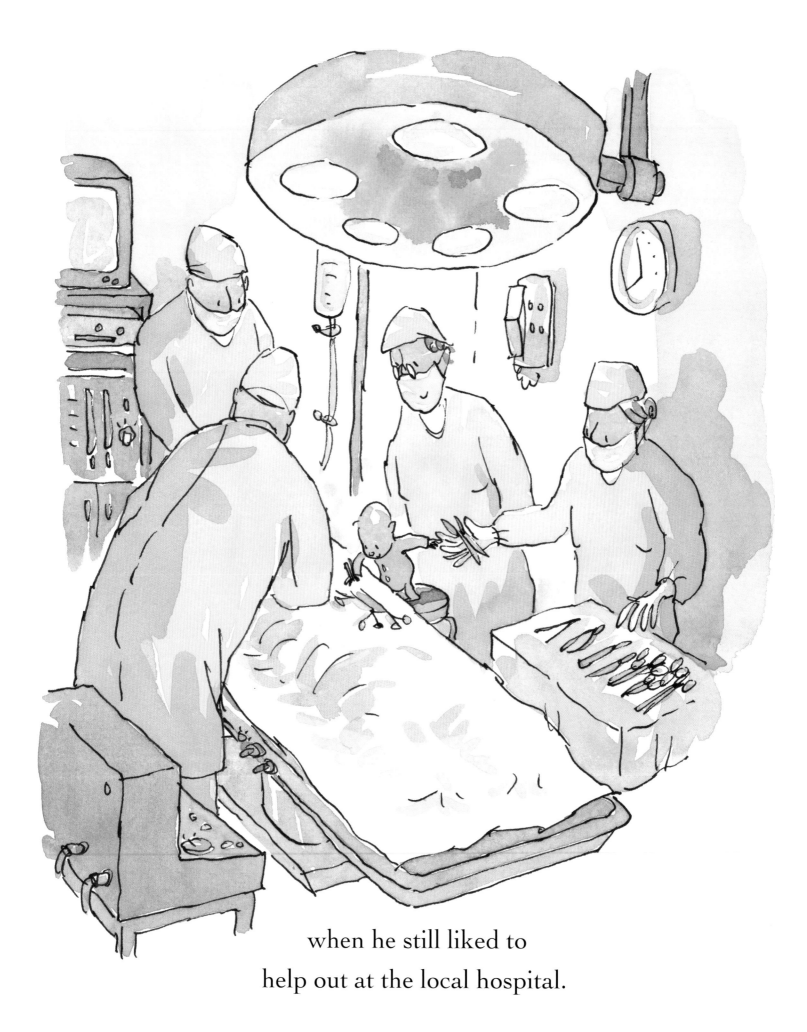

when he still liked to
help out at the local hospital.